CW00686970

SURFING

the 2020 anthology
of poetry and prose

by members of

the Federation of Writers (Scotland)

Published 2020
by New Voices Press
imprint of the Federation of Writers (Scotland)

www.federationofwritersscotland.wordpress.com

ISBN 978-1-906708-22-1

All rights reserved. No part of this book may be reproduced, stored in a retrieval system, or transmitted in any form or by any means (electronic, mechanical, photocopy, sound or digital recording) or translated into any language, without prior written permission from the Federation of Writers (Scotland), except by a reviewer who may quote brief passages in a review.

The rights of all contributors to be identified as the authors of their work in this book have been asserted by them in accordance with section 77 of the UK Copyright, Designs and Patents Act 1988.

Clip art courtesy of MariaFresa.net

Patrons

Dave Anderson	Carol Ann Duffy	Bashabi Fraser
Magi Gibson	Liz Lochhead	Christine de Luca
Carl MacDougall	Donny O'Rourke	Zoe Strachan
	Rosemary Ward	

	Makars	**Scrievers**
2008:	A C Clarke	-
2009:	Robin Cairns	-
2010:	Maggie Rabatski	-
2011:	Colin Will	-
2012:	Sheila Templeton	-
2013:	Rab Wilson	-
2014:	Anne Connolly	-
2015:	Brian Whittingham	-
2016:	Elizabeth Rimmer	-
2017:	Andy Jackson	-
2018:	Marjorie Lotfi Gill	-
2019:	Stephen Watt	Olga Wojtas
2020:	Finola Scott	Charlie Gracie

Introduction

In a year when the Covid-19 pandemic forced the world out of its routine and coerced people to find a new groove, a title such as *Surfing* implies one is still moving, kinetic, keeping a balance through life's obstacles and obstructions.

This collection tackles the waves of nostalgia — of lost youth — and the tempests of dementia. It steadies itself in the flow of Scotland's most bewitching locations, from Leith to Mull, Jura to Auchterarder. When our home country is not enough to soothe the soul, there are eagles, oystercatchers, the moon and stars magic-carpeting our readers to places of history, war, cruelty and love. These are the stormy verses wherein writers beg the Goddess of Calm Seas to quell the rage of the currents threatening to devastate their vessels. Provocative language sits on rocks like sirens, singing about independence and sectarianism; for or against?

Moments of jubilation permit the reader to breathe and regroup, sail on rippling smiles and fresh winds. There are stories and poems of classical music in budget hotels, concrete poetry in the shape of kites, the sweet release of music and dancing; the sweet release of holographic tombstones! I found myself revelling in the ludicrous notion of Prime Ministerial peer pressure and capital punishment; or is that really such a farcical whim? We surf on. Recognition of hospitals, the NHS, and all the mortal lives which travel through her swing doors. New-borns. Scans. The final goodbye. There is true introspection between these pages, considering our place and our purpose in this world.

To all intents and purposes, this collection oscillates. As reassuring as it is impactive, Surfing achieves the right balance of despair and sensation, agitation and aspiration. These poems and stories will throw you overboard and then as quickly offer a paddle back to safety. And like all quality collections, these will remain inside you in the days after, simmering just below the surface, begging the question: do the circling fins belong to dolphins or sharks?

Stephen Watt
July 2020

Acknowledgements:
Anne Connolly *for anthology team leadership*
Janet Crawford *for co-ordinating the submissions process*
Emma Mooney *for prose selections*
Neil Leadbeater *for poetry selections*
Sheila Templeton *for Scots writing selections*
Jenifer Harley *for production and distribution*
C Baker at drumcrosspublishing.com *for cover design*
Stephen Watt *for his generous comments on 'Surfing'*

SURFING

Writers

SURFING

Kirsten MacQuarrie

Miss Mew

"**N**ew?"
　"Mew."
"Mute?"
"Mew," I repeat the repetition.

"Ah, Miss Mew." The man — I refuse to call him gentle — experiments with rolling my name around his mouth, thick tongue flipping over each letter as if deciding whether or not he likes the taste. Bitter? It might well be.

"And you write little poems, do you Miss? Shining bright in our literary firmament these days, or so I'm told by Thomas..."

If I had forgotten — and I rarely forget things — then this man would be the perfect reminder of why I no longer attend parties. As he speaks, I allow my eyes to slide out of focus, drawn away from his pompous, port-reddled face and towards the closed velvet curtains beyond. Their sheer opulence is almost oppressive, tumbling down to cover the large-paned windows in a plush waterfall sweep. On either side of the expanse, gilt candlesticks stand guard like sentries. There will be no escaping tonight. At least not until after dinner is served.

"*'As the stars that shall be bright when we are dust, moving in marches across the heavenly plain...'* Now that's poetry for you. Those brave boys with their beautiful words." Reluctantly, I return my attention to my companion, now quoting from what is surely the single poem he knows by heart. We all know it. We have since 1918. "What do you write about, Miss Mew?" He leans forward conspiratorially. Breath hot; eyes sharp. "Had a sweetheart once, did you?"

"I..." Seldom am I lost for words. But which words to choose? How could I convey to this man that there is worth in what I write? Markets and beggars. Farmers and trees. When I speak of loss, it is not of the soldiers to whom monuments are made. It is of the tiny child who lives and dies without ever knowing a world beyond her sickbed. It is the loss of hope. Of faith. Or that quiet anguish of a loss which society forbids us even to mention. The loss of a mind when the body remains.

"Come now, sir, you have heard *The Farmer's Bride*?" Impressively attuned to signs of discord amongst her guests, Florence glides across the room to arrive at my side. She truly is the perfect hostess. The florid fellow appears to swell up: no, it transpires, he does not know the farm bride — "Farmer," Florence corrects him gently — and nor does he wish to.

8

"'Three summers since I chose a maid,
Too young maybe — but more's to do
At harvest-time than bide and woo.'"

Florence recites my opening verse as if it were a minor-key melody, her light voice animated by emotion.

"'When us was wed she turned afraid
Of love and me and all things human;
Like the shut of a winter's day
Her smile went out.'"

She halts. "Just think of it: a new wife caught and trapped, poorly matched to a husband who will never understand her mind. Tragic, sir, is it not?"

The ungentleman raises an eyebrow. The furrows of his plump forehead quickly absorb it. "Well, Miss Mew, perhaps we can agree on something," he concedes gruffly. "Woman rarely recognises the good fortune of her station."

"On the contrary, sir. I find most women know exactly how lucky they are."

*

"Eat, drink and be merry, my friends!" Mr Hardy calls down to us from the head of his table, sonorous and subtly commanding as at any literary performance. The dining room, like the salon, is decorated lavishly, if a little more Victorian in style than I suspect Florence herself would choose. A further brace of straight-backed candlesticks has been stationed along the table, supporting wax pillars that serve to flatter the complexions of the company with a uniform cast of gold. Does Florence use electricity when she is alone here? Is she ever alone here?

In front of me lies the full complement of silverware that befits a London dinner party and before the first course I catch sight of my reflection, convexed and contorted in the nearest filigree spoon. My face is pale. Angular. Watchful. When I look up again, uncomfortably conscious of the indigo circles haunting my eyesockets and cheekbones, Mr Hardy is smiling. He looks encouragingly in my direction, the way I imagine a father might coax an unathletic young boy up to the crease. He is kind to me. So too, of course, is Florence, although tonight I

9

sense that she is strained by something beyond the pressures of society entertainment. Their townhouse is impressive, imposing even, but surely their souls also crave a retreat to his mythical Wessex? On paper at least, if not in person. There are too many humans here. Too few trees. A new fashion for cutting them down — the trees, not the humans — is upon us and the brutality of it burns me, painfully corrosive as if I had swallowed poison. What makes man so certain that because something — someone — is trapped in silence, they cannot feel suffering? I start scribbling out a line, murmuring to myself as the sounds of a new poem take root. "Grate." "Swish." "Crash." "Fall." In lieu of a proper pen, I carve the words into a napkin with the raw edge of my fingernail.

"Miss Mew?" Concerned faces are peering along the table. Peppered in a few places with poorly stifled sniggers. Odd, isn't she? Is she mad?

"We were talking about the franchise." The colour in my new acquaintance's cheeks is sinking deeper with every glass of wine he drinks. What were once dots of puce have now spread, spilling out into two blotchy blooms of purple. "First they grant it to women —"

"Some women," Florence quietly amends.

"Who next? Lunatics?" The man guffaws at his own suggestion. "Not that there's always a difference between the two!"

I clench my napkin tighter inside my fist, called to courage as my fingers find the faintly etched imprint of my words. "I think a woman no longer in her right mind was likely driven from it by men."

*

After dinner, the sexes part company. The gentlemen retire to the parlour, eager to enjoy their whisky and cigars, while the ladies indulge their own equally thrilling vice of gossip. Florence, as ever, has prepared well for the moment. When we enter the drawing room, I see that silver bowls filled with confectionery await us on every glossed side table. The nearest offering is pear drops. A favourite. Checking that nobody is watching, I gather up a handful of the pastel-hued sweets, wrapping them inside my napkin as a reminder to keep them safe. When finally I take my seat on a high-backed chair — the chaises longues have already been claimed by women quicker off the mark — it is a challenge to feign interest in the conversation. The group's most confident characters regale us with tales of their latest household dramas, the plots of which hang invariably upon lace, lost gloves and insubordinate kitchen maids.

"Serving red wine? With fish? Is she insane?"

Midway through proceedings, Florence excuses herself, murmuring about the need to thank her housekeeper before the evening's end. I do not hesitate to

10

take my chance. Unnoticed and unmissed, I slip outside. Even a London garden is more comforting than none. The hedges are high, diamond-leaf tendrils of ivy coiling over the iron gates, and at the far end of the lawn, a single tree stands proud. I should have known Mr Hardy would not allow his to be felled. Its winter branches twist in the wind, phantom fingers tickling the night air as if trying to touch the moon. I can discern, if only just, the small black mass that denotes a bird's nest. The fledgling family can no longer be in residence, their infants surely grown and taken to the skies several months ago. Yet I am drawn to the thought that they linger nearby, watching me through the shadows as I seek the same sanctuary they once did. When close enough, I press my forehead to the tree trunk. Cool. Coarse. Comforting. As I lean, a hairpin is dislodged, and I allow the loosened strands of brown hair to mingle with the bark.

"Charlotte." Can I trust him? Is he the Tom who understood Tess: that rare man who intuited the sorrow felt exclusively by women, bound inside stone circles of fate from which we never seem to break free? Or is he the Mr Hardy who took a lover forty years his junior: humiliating his late wife and now, in the eternal spirit of employment creating a vacancy, humiliating Florence too? His hand grazes my own. My pulse beats beneath his fingers.

"Clever little Charlotte. Are you well, my dear?" A rogue lock falls over my face and he brushes it away. Palm pressed against my cheek.

Like the shut of a winter's day
Her smile went out.

"Quite well, sir. But it is time for me to go."

*

When I leave, I walk. Averting my eyes from Florence's concern — and fending off the bizarre offer of a taxicab shared with my flush-faced adversary — I set off on foot along the pavement. To travel alone feels grounding, allaying my fears that a car or, even worse, conversation will jostle the nascent rhythm of my poem out my head. I think of the napkin and am tempted to check it, but I know that the roughly inscribed words will be invisible until I find better light. A few right (or wrong) turns and the true darkness of the city engulfs me. There are no gilt candleholders here. No velvet and often no curtains either. The railings are blackened not by paint but street grime, and from a bird's eye view I imagine the decay around me: pockmarking parts of the city where post-war progress is yet to reach. Yes, its people survived, but for what? Not always a life worth living.

The nurse is slow to answer the door.

"Late for you, Miss Mew. You've missed dinnertime."

"How is…?"

"Settled. And safer down here, I'm sure. We don't want another attempt." She turns away to rearrange a pile of thin blankets, pressing the material down firmly as if it recently caused her offence. The new room is downstairs — after the incident, views went from being a right to a privilege — and I take each tread cautiously, mindful of how easily a loud footstep can startle. There is a window here, albeit one cut from clouded glass. As I descend, all I can see is the kerbside. Ill-defined blocks of black? The thick boots of passing men. Darting slivers of shadow? The feet of children, hurrying past the asylum.

"Freda."

Nothing.

"Freda."

I pause.

"Sister."

Freda blinks, then continues to stare ahead. There are scratches on her arms from before they cut her nails. Patches of raw, pulled scalp from before they cut her hair. Auburn, it was. Auburn and beautiful. Unfurling the napkin, I offer Freda the pear drops. At first, she does not seem to react, but then with a soft rippling movement her fingers start to reach for them. Tentative and weak, but reaching nonetheless. At the first taste of sweetness, she gives a half smile. I half smile, too. I take her hand in my own and, slowly, feel her skin growing warmer. Her eyelids fall. Head droops. Limbs loosen. Freda dozes and I write, concluding the lines that I began elsewhere.

> *They are cutting down the great plane-trees at the end of the gardens.*
> *For days there has been the grate of the saw, the swish of the branches as they fall,*
> *The crash of the trunks, the rustle of trodden leaves,*
> *With the 'Whoops' and the 'Whoas', the loud common talk, the loud common laughs of the men, above it all.*
>
> [from *'The Trees are Down'* by Charlotte Mew]

Sam Smith

A dark wing brushed her mind, leaving a pause; a blank space.
(Virginia Woolf: 'The Years')

Within the house, treading day's routines room to room, forgetfulness accuses her of obscure errors. (As if there was a way of getting the whole of a life right.) Nor does the small garden offer the refuge of distraction: perpetual rustle of roadside poplars, constant tyre-scratch of traffic, along with the throat-coo back-and-forth of the rookery; all feels to be squashing her. And it's no better when the jolly women call, seek to 'involve her'; but spend so long deferring one to another that they decide late where to go, if at all. Although once out and about, bench sat, and left quietly to herself, she enjoys taking in the small tableaux and pleasures of ordinary people. Not in a patronising way, more as an aide memoire to her own once happy times.

Donald Saunders

A Grandson

For newborn Billy
my little finger is a handful.

He tests this
frail limb of the family tree

and I feel again the grip
the child his father had,

daring to hope to see
the day when he can

take my whole hand
and I, in kindred correspondence, his.

Sharon Collins

A Map of Tiny Shores

And so we return to our tiny shores
Europeans, naw, no anymore
I thought we'd moved beyond our tiny shape
into a European landscape
I was part of something bigger
who worked and traded and moved freely together
but it seems it didn't matter whether
I voted for or against this divorce
Scotland had no say in it of course!

Adieu adieu Nineteen-Seventy-Two
from those Eton boys who pledge and vow
to have bolted up our borders now
and made 'Great' Britain safe again
from European tyrants and all those migrants
and that surgeon who saved my father's life
our borders cut with a Tory knife
and so we return to our tiny shores
Europeans, naw, no anymore

Our nation's history we can rewrite
in the spirit of our Jacobite
a rebellion still of 'Forty-Five
for bonnie Scotland who will survive
beyond our map of tiny shores
Europeans, naw, no anymore!

Dipper
for Honor

As if it had been hit with a snowball
right in the middle of its chest
and couldn't be bothered removing it,
we saw the dipper standing there
looking at us from its stone perch
on the Water of Leith
and with a nonchalant bravado
it dived into the cold waters
and disappeared for what seemed ages.

Its reappearance had you hopping
with the excitement of youth
and we watched it several times
doing what it does naturally.
It was probably showing off
for it had such a captive audience
with your squeals of approval
and before we left we had strangely
organised another audience
to take our place beside the wall.

That dipper had entered your being
because later there was a barrier
that had to be negotiated
further on the path upstream.
You climbed the barrier no problem
but wanted to jump down
instead of using nearby steps.
The sixty something granny you are
became a twenty someone else
with years slipped away like a dipper
diving head on into a rushing river.

Paula Nicolson

Beats On Repeat

The beats build fast and crescendo through my body; intensity rising from feet to head like a wave shoaling to the shore. BOOM! I'm tipping my head and arms backwards: surrendering. Pure adrenaline, kicked in by copious tequila shots served by a cowgirl with shaky hands. It burns as it slips down my throat; my confidence-inducing nectar, work your magic, please.

This is what I've come for: the beats. Repetitive, mixed with a sampled track. A kaleidoscope of notes and emotions. Over and over again they play; beats on repeat. RAVE! My body twists with the rhythm, my wet hair underneath my fringe to see if he's watching; he is. Then I smile and twist slapping my cheeks as I shake my head from side to side. I peer from into carefully coordinated, choreographed shapes: I'm a peacock ready for a pick-up. Tussling through the bouncer's petty dress code checks, a snatched crumpled fiver to get in, and then pissing in front of women in a doorless toilet, was all worth it.

I can beat all the bad boyfriends, the rent, the shit day at work. DANCE! I'm in ecstasy without taking any. I'm in heaven without being an angel. I can take on the world without leaving the club. My sweat trickles between my shoulder blades as he pulls me close. His kiss tastes salty, his lips soft, yet needy. Mmmm — he smells good too: Mr Sophisticated-On-A-Stick.

I never want this kiss, this track, this dance to end. Please, beats on repeat.

Derek Crook

Winter at Uisken Beach

The wind wakes weed-scabbed sand,
stirs it, hisses it against sere stalks.
Grains stumble as drunks do at dawn.

One white feather
footfast in sandtrap
sways in impotent silence.

The grey sea plots.

Where I would see
in summer the shimmer
of water, the white winking
of surf on the reef,
hear the chatter of wavelets and birds
and of children
there is now
only drab reference.

And memories.
Yes, of course. There are memories.

It's not, no it's not the surges of spring
I long for,
the creaking of husks
wrapped round dry seeds
nor wisps of grass hanging from birdbeak
nor an autumn of berries on blackthorn or rowan
or briars reddening, stiffening and arching
or greylag geese waving slow wings of goodbye.

No, now I dream of
summer's serenity, fields of
fully formed flowers
footed in green,
of succulence under blue skies

of lark hallelujas
and you.

To Heather

Greg Michaelson

Galatea

You seek to treat me other than I am,
as if I were a lumpen block of Spam,
fearful and trembling for your shameless knife,
that carves crude, sensate, Golem-globs of life.

Coax me, wheedle, deprecate and flatter;
slice me up and lather me in batter.
Tolling the deep fat fryer's bubbling knell;
encase me in your crisp protective shell.

Pink and naked, lurking deep within,
yearning yet for my dark embracing tin.
Am I for eating? Am I for discourse?
Gone in a bite, or plate-bound, wreathed in sauce?

Love is more than a gourmand's escapade.
You be my Spam; I'll be your marinade.

Beth McDonough

Oystercatchers and Myopia

Let me love them for their well-drawn lines,
black and white patterns, even startled in flight.
Long-beaked turf inspectors.

Let me love them for sharp orange beaks,
up-down dips in water, or into dun sand.
Inland improvers of verges.

Let me love them for that skinny limb poise,
upholding a Beardsley-penned body.
Their beak and leg bright colour zing.

Let me love them for thripping at chicks,
then for high skyfuls of wheeples.
That quiet attention to worms.

Most of all, let me love them in unnumbered ways
for the blurred joy they give when I learn
they're not the wrong number of magpies.

David McVey
Flagship Policy

Ooh, scones! Marvellous! Pour us a coffee, will you, Brian?
Now, Brian, just before your meeting with the Azerbaijani ambassador, I thought I'd bring you up to speed on the policy proposal that we raised last week. The meeting to move it forward is tomorrow. Come on, you remember; we nicknamed it Operation Long Drop?

Look, take it easy, Brian, just listen, will you? I know what I'm talking about. You're only the Prime Minister, you just had to be *elected*. I'm *qualified* to be your confidential policy advisor. So when I recommend...

What? Look, I've told you before, I've got a BA in Political and Policy Advice from the University of Central Northumberland. By distance learning. Yes, I know that you ponced about at Edinburgh and Oxford and Princeton but what career does *Philosophy* prepare you for, least of all politics? I, on the other hand, am qualified to advise you. The whole policy team, and most of the cabinet, are convinced that this one's a winner.

Yes, Brian, I'm well aware that our official policy opposes capital punishment. What you and the party just don't get is that when we propose reintroducing public hangings we're emphasising the *public* not the *hanging*. It's not really about punishment or crime or anything sordid. No, it's about strengthening community, boosting the economy, bringing back the feelgood factor. Frequent hanging fairs will give the people regular parties, something they can go to with their mates, take the kids, socialise with the neighbours. They'll want food, drink, sideshows, entertainment, transport to and from the hanging and so whole industries will spring up just to cater for them. And that's before you start manufacturing ropes and scaffolds and employing local joiners to build platforms and, er, trapdoors and things.

Oh, don't be such an old woman, Brian. This isn't the fifties, people aren't squeamish any more. Every film, every streaming boxset you see now has slashing, slicing, dicing, shooting, bombing, evisceration, sexual violence all in close-up and slow-mo and 3D. Someone being hanged is just good old-fashioned family entertainment compared to films and games and TV. And the ones who watch hostage execution videos on YouTube will love it.

I take your point, Brian; it is a bit disconcerting to think that those sickos will be in the crowd when you go along innocently to watch a nice public hanging. But we'll make sure the events are well-policed. Yes, the cops are quite keen on it all. More overtime, a rare chance to see the conclusion of the judicial process, all that.

'Wrong'? Oh, stop being so prissy, Brian, I'm fed up with your Baptist upbringing and your dreary trade unionist uncles. I keep telling you — a social conscience is a serious handicap in politics. This is what society wants, it's what the market wants; all we're doing is listening to the people. And the left of the party is quite happy, too, now that we've assured them that public hangings won't be privatised. All the profits stay in the public purse and local councils will be able to raise money through street trading, public entertainment licences and venue hire. Everybody wins. Well, no, Brian, I suppose not absolutely everybody, not the fellow dangling on the end of the rope, I accept that, but you see my point, surely?

There will be a dividend for the whole country, with public hangings in every town and city. Of course, the Jocks are being stroppy as usual: 'We've got our own poxy little legal system and you can't make us hang people.' Moving troops across the border like we did over the independence nonsense should bring them into line. What? Of course I know you're from Scotland, Brian, I just thought you'd outgrown that sort of thing now that you're here in London.

Yes, we'll keep all the showpiece executions in London but we haven't decided on a venue, yet. Wembley and Stamford Bridge are keen, and there's a good case for Trafalgar Square, but the Tower seems to be the obvious place. We've already come up with a slogan — 'Hanging's Coming Home!' Do you see what we did there?

There's no need for language like that, Brian. Your old Sunday School teacher would be shocked to hear it. Sorry, what's that? Well, yes, we'd have to make quite a range of crimes into capital offences, just to keep up the supply side. Murder, attempted murder, manslaughter, culpable — whatever that Scottish one is, assault, burglary, car theft. There's been a suggestion that Members of Parliament who fiddle their expenses should be hanged since that would guarantee huge crowds... No, calm down, Brian, it's just a suggestion at this stage.

So, d'you feel fully briefed for the meeting? Just think about it, Brian. I'm sure you'll come round. The papers love it, especially *The Sun*, the *Express*, and the *Mail*, of course, they've already inquired about sponsorship. The *Telegraph* is being a bit coy — cautious welcome as long as we 'implement appropriate safeguards'. The *Mirror* is apopleptic but... Oh, don't be ridiculous, Brian, nobody reads *The Guardian*. We've also had good feedback from the public and businesses. Churches and community groups are bleating a bit but we can just threaten to tax them if they stay awkward.

No, I don't agree at all, Brian. This will be your great Flagship Policy; wins elections, good for business, popular, reduces the prison population, fights crime and takes people's minds off the fact that they're unemployed or poor or living in a damp house surrounded by pinch-faced neighbours with killer dogs. Everything about your life seems better when you've just seen some other wretch get his neck snapped.

Oh, before the meeting, there are some papers for you to read and videos to watch, comparing different hanging technologies. No, nothing too graphic. I don't think so, anyway. But you'll have to get used to it, you know, you'll be expected to attend the first of the new public hangings — and to show some bloody *enthusiasm*.

Just one more thing to run past you and see what you think. A few people have suggested extending the policy to introduce public *beheadings*... Oh, quick, get a cloth, coffee can be murder to get out of suit trousers. That's it, you can change before you meet the ambassador and that can go to the cleaners'.

Yes, beheading has become quite cool, with all those Islamic extremist execution videos posted online. There's a feeling that mere hangings might be a bit tame for that market. Something to think about, anyway. I wonder if anyone still manufactures scimitars in this country — Sheffield perhaps? I'll get the research boys onto it.

Well, thanks for your time, Brian, make sure you get that suit cleaned. I'll see you at the cabinet meeting after you've met the ambassador. Mind if I have the last of these scones? Ta. Really need to think about dieting, but meanwhile I might as well be hung for a pound as a penny, eh?

See you later, Brian.

Paula Nicolson

The Railway Man

He was a railway man through and through, before the war.
He built the carriages to run across God's country.
They said he could be a medic; a saver of lives, not a killer.
Left behind from a precipice assault: a remote Japanese island that even his
    geography teacher never knew existed.
Facing an enemy, he couldn't see.
His skin prickled with the heat.
The smell of charred bodies clung to his uniform.
The cries of the injured had become his new best friend.
He remembers the satisfying slam of train doors and the reek of used
    engine oil.
Japanese prisoners built railway lines; bodies buried alongside the sleepers.
No sleep for him.
It was time to tell the dead they were loved; eyes shut for the last time.
To hold the hands of the wounded; whisper they'd see their loved ones
    soon.
To drag the saved to the cliff edge, and with rope tied to their tired bodies,
    lower one by one; just like broken down train carriages.
Ready to be repaired.
He was still a railway man, through and through.

*Note: This poem is loosely based on the bravery of US Army Corporal Desmond Doss in
saving 75 men on the Maeda Escarpment (Hacksaw Ridge) in the Battle of Okinawa, 1945.*

Marie Isabel Matthews-Schlinzig

Beginning

what does she see
when she first looks
at me

while I myself
think of ourselves
as one

outside the window
snow is falling

thick cottony and soft
on leafless trees
on lamplit streets
on roofs of houses and
on parking cars

the pain of birthing
lingers
still

having no laughter yet
I sneeze

stick out my tongue
maybe
to catch a flake
or two

now everything is new

For Niamh

Buoyancy

You tell me
I carry too much
and you're right — mother's
weekly shopping her puzzled shadow that
telephones at 1a.m. her locket round my neck
engraved by nine year old teeth (she started young)
my children from the day they were born over a hundred
and seventy six kilos between them my father in law on his
hospital bed the birds waiting to be fed every morning quieter
and hungrier than before and I still haven't read *The Unbearable
Lightness of Being* so you tell me to let it go as we watch this rusting
and decrepit battle-cruiser yaw to windward too low in the water
which is not surprising what with the millions of dying bees
swarming on the mast and the entire Vatnajökull Glacier
melting through the deck while from the stern that
woman who keeps texting to tell me meat
is murder and wants to go for coffee
some time gives me a passive
aggressive wave just
before they slip
over the
horizon
I shrug
what
can
you
do,
our
arms
twist together
buck
like
kite
strings,
we
kiss,
close
our
eyes,
drift
up.

Ross McWhinnie

Castlebay

I can see her from the roadside.
The wind is on her breath
wheezing in creels long stashed and rotting
snorting in barrels whose brackish catch
of rain and rust pollutes
concrete.

Twice a day she comes
to gnaw the shore's knuckle
at the place rough fingers ran
through her rougher mane of ropes
and forgot
the cold of her deep meadow,
her black stable.

A buoy flashes.
Gale is spliced to tide.
Gulls share all this and do not care.

Everything is half-finished.

Lynn Valentine

Golden Eagles above Jura

We spotted four of them,
a gyre of muscle and wing,
high cries looping out to the Sound and back again

circling above Barnhill, shadows breaking
on the roof and fields. We talked of Orwell,
how the world seemed doomed decades on

and yet we couldn't break
our gaze from this soaring,
this upward draft of gold and song.

Mary Nixon

Guinness

We've got a new book called The Guinness Book of Records. I grabbed it first and started looking for things like — the oldest teacher, the smelliest feet, the hairiest mole, but there's nobody in it we know. That new boy Ewan says there's somebody that's a hundred and forty but that's rubbish.

Even the teacher said, "I don't think so."

Angela looked up the bit about the tallest people and there's somebody that's as big as Goliath in The Bible. The pictures are brilliant and there's lots of weird stuff like the longest nails and the biggest number of bee stings taken out of somebody.

Billy McFall wants to know if there's any records for farting and the teacher says, "No but there's a record for the densest objects. That should interest you."

I think he'd win it for smelliest farts but how can you measure those?

"Please Miss could we try a new record?" says Angela.

"Well," says the teacher, sort of slow like she's thinking about it. "There's the Fun Day coming up soon. Maybe we could do a record of sorts. I'll add that to my list."

Me and Angela were organising the netball shooting. That's our best talent. Big Wullie's down for Beat the Goalie cause he just about fills the net and he's that annoying everybody wants to beat him or batter him with the ball.

Then Billy McFall reads about a record for eating beans with chopsticks, and that starts him off again, "Beans beans are good for your heart, the more you eat —"

"Stop right there," said the teacher. "We'll have none of your toilet humour in here."

My granny said she could get us a loan of a wooden wall thing with a hole your head goes through for people to throw wet sponges. A lot of the boys said they'd take shots to go in it. The teacher said she'd ask Mr Younger if he'd take a shot. That would make a fortune.

The teacher brought in a big jar of sweeties that somebody gave her. You had to guess how many were in the jar. She wanted volunteers to count them. I volunteered first and she said me and Angela could stay in at lunch time and do it. We had to wash our hands and the teacher left paper plates to put the sweets on in bundles of ten to make it easy.

We had eight plates of ten when Angela said, "What part of the jelly baby do you eat first?"

I always bite the head off first but she does feet first. That's daft.

"You try the feet and I'll do the head for a change," she said. So we did. Then we started biting the arms off first. Then I tried to bite the belly buttons. That was tricky. We stopped and counted what was left — sixty six — and the jar was half empty.

"You know what the teacher says," said Angela. "If you're an optimist jars aren't half empty, they're half full."

I laughed that much, I nearly choked on my last jelly baby. We didn't think the teacher would be laughing when she found out. I had this sick feeling. Angela thought it was the sugar. We put the jar in at the back of the cupboard and piled stuff in front of it.

My granny thought it was hilarious. She went to the shops the next day for more sweets and we smuggled them into the jar at playtime when we were locking the door.

The teacher said Billy could use a cocktail stick for the beans to make it easier but he said, "That's pure rubbish. My da's went and got me chopsticks specially. He said it might be in the paper."

That was cos my granny had spoken to the man from The Gazette. He's been trying to work his way up to The Daily Record ever since my granny delivered the baby in the high flats. There was a big headline all with capital letters on the front page.

"I'll be sure to tell him about the beans," she said. "If he's lucky he'll be standing upwind."

The dinner ladies put cold baked beans on paper plates for the four boys that were going to do the challenge. They said there was two hundred on each plate. They said they had a method of counting them so everyone got the same amount. Sarah was helping in the kitchen and said it was just a big tin of beans dolloped on each paper plate. We couldn't get anybody from The Guinness Book to verify it. That means they check it out. But the man from The Gazette and his photo guy were going to write a story with lots of pictures of the Fun Day.

The plates were lined up on a long table in the playground. There were cards with the boys' names in front of each plate. Miss McTavish had a stop watch cos they only got thirty seconds. Only three boys turned up — Billy, Stevie and Wee Sammy.

The teacher said, "Ready boys. Remember you can't lift your cocktail stick till the whistle goes."

31

And she blew it. Billy shouts after the first bean, "They're cold. I don't like cold beans!"

Then he sees Stevie getting stuck in and he stops moaning and tries to go faster than him. Sammy was going great as well till the teacher shouts, "Fifteen seconds left!" Then he got up and ran across the playground to the toilets. The other two kept going. The teacher shouts, "Ten," and we all join in, "nine, eight, seven, six, five, four, three, two, one, zero!" and the whistle blew.

Billy stood up waving his arms and Stevie sicked up all the beans he'd ate back onto the plate. Yuk!

Billy was the winner and the dinner ladies took his plate so they could count how many beans he'd ate.

Says my granny, "Do you know that game, Think of a Number?"

I was in charge of the money for the netball shooting. If you scored three times you got three more shots. Big deal. At least at the tombola you could win a bottle of something. There was whisky and gin and wine. My granny and mum won a ginormous bottle of vinegar, coconut shampoo, a bottle of beer and the biggest bottle of tomato ketchup you've ever seen in your whole life. It could have got in The Guinness Book of Records.

I went round the stalls just before the end. I got a lolly in the treasure hunt, a pen set in the lucky dip, tablet at the cake and candy stall and some tries on the raffles. I guessed the doll's birthday was the same as mine but I never took a shot of the sweeties in the jar cos I knew the number and I'm sick of jelly babies.

The best bit was the wet sponges. I got Mr Younger twice and Wullie four times. Angela got Billy McFall six times and you never knew if he was farting cos his bum was round the back. We were skint but it was worth it.

It turned out Billy had read the book wrong — it should have been chopsticks and jelly beans!

Mandy Macdonald

Listening to Vivaldi in a Premier Inn

waiting for you again

strings shiver and keen
sound circumnavigates
purple and white, buzzing

but this is not a field of lupins
by any stretch, this is not the zing
of insect polyphony

ninth-floor window bolted shut

no exit for errant semiquavers
or suicides, no saffron strands
of longing

can escape to find you
guide you to me
in this faux-ivory tower

Kathryn Metcalfe

No One Ever Sees Their Last Sunset

Into the conch of your ear
I will whisper yours

wait until the priest with his purple stole
anoints with prayers and balsam
slips away like a thief in the night

then I can tell you

how winter is reluctant to leave
April to the trust of spring
snow still cross-hatches beyond
the hospice window
a trace of silver rimes
the pale egg shell sky

now the sun ebbs steadily
to the edge of the horizon
marbling the clouds
with shades of rose and gold

until it purples to the deep navy
of those biblical scenes
where the Magi travel
across a darkening desert

they are waiting there
those wise men
where the dark meets the dawn.

Joe Murray

Oor Ane Licht (Sleat)

It cams back tae us frae oot thi daurk.
Paintins, faces, your smile, reflectit;
daunce on the ither side o thi windae
ower thi Sound that grabbles and cheeps
as it rowes ayont the hiddly shore ablow.
It is nae thi wine or thi beer
or thi crack or thi cheer
that cuitles thi fantice —
ideas o ethereal dreams
frae shaidaes on windaes —
but kenin that same licht
that dances, tapsalteerie,
frae oot that same daurk
endures atween you and me.

Glossary:

grabbles	=	*grasps*
cheeps	=	*whispers*
rowes	=	*rolls*
ayont	=	*beyond*
hiddly	=	*invisible*
cuitles	=	*prompts*
fantice	=	*imagination*
shaidaes	=	*shadows*
kenin	=	*knowing*
tapsalteerie	=	*head-over-heels, topsyturvy*

David Bleiman

Rewilding the Zoo

A great spotted woodpecker knocks

a black and white badger burrows

carrion crows fearlessly feast
among the cassowaries

herring gulls circle and swoop
on children's chips

pigeons from town peck
at leavings of pot-bellied pigs

a zebra or panda crossing
at the entrance gate

each species
draws the line somewhere

animal man
sapient Scottish zoological
drew a line across Corstorphine hill.

Hot day at the Holiday Inn
in a conference room at the back
open the windows to let in a breeze

here in our hearing a witness
stops
sobbing softly

the chimps set off screeching
and we all start laughing then
stop

hands on mouths
knowing
someone has crossed the line.

Mora Maclean

Scan

I'm entering in good faith; being slickly
drawn into the narrow tunnelled bulk, to lie
within a heartbeat of myself. The tilt of a tiny
mirror just above preserves, beyond my feet,
the room's still breathable space.

As headphones faintly stream the CD
I brought — to preclude the signature torture
of Adele, James Blunt et al, a sudden buzz — urgent,
visceral — comes pulsating through the fuzz,
births a gamut of whirrs, beeps, clangs —

the machine working up a right percussive
funk. Amidst all the Sturm und Drang,
I drift: envisage, on their screen, expanding
cross-sections of thought, queerly slowing
the flow of my thinking; a lattice for capturing

love — all kinds lighting up the grid;
something indistinct slinking opaquely
through, now nosing under my hand,
into all my supposed supposing.
Afterwards, dressing again, I button

up the sensation of hackles —
spiking from the spine; and shuttling
along on the express bus back — thrawn,
between memory and bone — something
that won't leave the heart alone.

Danny Murphy

Just One Punch

It was all down to one punch. And the best of it is I'd never thrown a punch in anger before, not in any of my fifty-five years. N. E. Never.

Don't get me wrong. I got into lots of scraps at school — 'toy fighting' we called it back in the day — but we didn't injure each other, just a bit of harmless wrestling. And I was never bullied — maybe because I was good at rugby? At five eight and eleven stone I wasn't the tallest or the strongest, but I was usually the fastest. Team mates used to compliment me on my killer tackles. "Weight's the least important part of the equation," I'd tell them. "Remember your Einstein?" I usually had to explain: "$E=mc^2$? — speed matters more than mass? Much more!" I'd say, in my smart-alec voice. "Much, much more!"

Neither punching nor punched — that was me: it'd never been my language. Until that wretched day in Money Merchants — pawn shops give themselves such fancy names these days, don't they?

I'd often seen it from the upper deck of the bus — but I'd never have gone in, obviously, if not for the deceptively simple request from my daughter, after she and her latest moved to Plymouth. "Dah-ahd?" she said — and when she uses that tone of voice I know that I'm already half way round her little finger — "Dah ahd? You know the stuff I left in the attic?"

Yes. I knew that stuff alright — old computer equipment, plastic covered dumbbells, a doll's house, a toy pram, her books and notes from Uni. Piles upon piles. None of it any use to me.

"I'm just wondering," she wheedled, "would you be able to sell them for me? The books can go to Oxfam, but the other stuff, you might get something for it at Money Merchants, or somewhere like that?"

Of course I would. Delighted to be useful. Scared to lose her, to be honest. Happy for any kind of contact. Any at all.

I wasn't going to take the actual items of course. Too many. Too bulky. But I did take an A4 page for each one — photo at the top, detailed specification below — 'so many gigaherz', 'duo processor', 'one careful owner', you know the kind of thing. I could always post anything they wouldn't take on eBay.

*

The website said the shop opened at 9.30. I arrived at 9.35 expecting it to be empty. What did I know? There was a stale earthy smell, like a recently occupied stable stall. I strolled past the bags of old golf clubs, shelves of used laptops, a selection of Xbox games, so much junk it's hard to believe anyone had ever wanted. "The sad detritus of failed consumerism," I thought, in what my nearest and dearest used to call 'my pompous manner'. In my defence you do get used to the sound of your own voice if you teach in a University. At home too. On my own now. When my good lady left me, she cited my 'supercilious tone of voice' as one of several 'aggravating factors'.

At the back of the shop, where the buying counters are, there was a queue of four or five people beside a couple of old diesel generators. I stood in line, trying to look as if I belonged, though Nicolson Square is far from the petits fours, fresh croissants and hand-roasted coffee of my side of Edinburgh. The service area needed a good lick of paint. The security camera hung limply, pointing at the floor, sticky tape over its broken lens. The assistants behind the counters were uninterested, their skin a pasty white from long hours of working indoors. The punters ahead of me looked like they'd spent the week's benefits already, just needed topped up for the weekend — a casting queue for a remake of Trainspotting.

One of them, a pint-sized citizen, was peering through the thick lenses of what looked like a pair of old national health specs. He was of indeterminate age, his face and neck spotty, his long greasy red hair and baggy black shellsuit completing the look of someone who'd time-shifted from the nineteen-eighties. He offered a loud commentary on his morning in an irritating nasal whine, as if we were his interested intimates. We heard about 'a baldy cunt' who pushed him at the bus stop, 'a wee fanny' who'd been at his school and was still 'a wee fanny' — ha, ha, ha. The previous night's football was then subjected to a pithy analysis: 'Rangers were fuckin lucky,' and Gerrard, he told us, was much given to onanism. I was aware — surprised even — that I was actually enjoying this unplanned social observation: there is another half, even so near to the University, and the queue in Money Merchants, I realised, provides the social voyeur with particularly rich material.

The counter assistant on the right pulled down the screen and headed into the back office, just as the wee fellow reached the front of the queue. He turned round and caught my eye. "Fuckin ridiculous this," he said. I wasn't too impressed either. It was already past ten. The queue at the other counter hadn't moved since I arrived: the same two customers. The one on the left was an older guy, maybe sixty. His bald head was used to the outdoors, an even demerara sugar colour running over and round its indentations and scars. He was restless, constantly fiddling with his chestnut-coloured walking stick and his gold earring. The other man was younger, a little taller, with the same sharp nose and chin. His son, I surmised. They'd been arguing with the assistant, intensely but all sotto voce. I could only make out an odd word or two — "...breakage... last time... you people..."

The wee guy suddenly turned to me and started shouting. "How long have we been fuckin waitin!" My nod betokened slight agreement but also a distinct lack of interest in taking up the case. "And there's only one fuckin counter open. Should be another wan oan," he railed. "I'm no hingin aboot here. I'm a busy guy." His complaint attracted murmurs of agreement from those behind. Thus emboldened, he stepped forward.

"Cin youse no hurry up, ay?" he said to the father and son — not, I thought, over-confrontationally. Indeed given his earlier language, this seemed beyond polite.

The bald gent turned round. "Whit is it to you, you wee cunt," he said.

"I wis jist sayin —"

"Whit?"

The wee guy said nothing, but his expression had changed. He showed fear. The old man saw it too. He threw away the stick and dived forward with a vicious right hook. The wee fellow's specs cracked, and a red weal was already developing on his temple before the second blow knocked him against the opposite wall. He adopted a crouching posture, covering his face.

"Dinny," he snivelled, "Ah nivir meant nothin."

The baldy gent's younger companion came over. I thought he was going to calm the situation when I saw him smiling, but he pulled the wee guy to his feet and pushed him towards the door. "Get tae the back o the queue, ya wee radge," he shouted, "an leave ma da alone."

There was no-one to hide behind now, and as the pair turned to resume their transaction, the old guy's eyes met mine. I acknowledge as a failing of mine that people think that I'm sometimes looking down my nose. Indeed my good wife often found occasion to remark that I was 'a smug know-it-all'. I could never mount a serious defence to that charge. I may not know it all, of course, but I really do know much — much much — more than most. It is also true, as she frequently remarked, that my face can be read like a book.

And, unfortunately for me, the old guy was a skilled reader of faces.

"Whit're you lookin at?" he said. The vein in his temple was throbbing, a powerful cocktail of high grade testosterone pumping through his system. I saw that splendid right hook coming.

It'd been a long time since I'd had to react that quickly, but I'm rather proud to say that I'd lost none of my speed. I deflected the blow harmlessly away with my left arm. He'd put so much effort into it that he overbalanced, stumbling towards me, and I delivered a fast right uppercut — extremely fast, even if I say so myself — to the point of his chin.

There was no dramatic sound, just a sudden soft thunk, but $E=mc^2$ — remember? — and there was plenty of c^2 in that punch. His head jerked and his knees collapsed, his upper body toppling backwards. I could immediately see what was going to happen. I think everyone watching probably saw it too. Time slowed — you may remember Einstein had something to say about that too — as he fell backwards onto one of the portable generators. When his skull crashed into the cooling fins of the cylinder there was a wet crunching sound and we could all see the blood oozing out onto the floor, bright red, viscous. Altogether shocking.

"What the fuck've you done?" the son shouted as he lunged towards me. I was no longer in fight mode and there was a strong case for flight, but from nowhere two massive arms encircled his waist and a man mountain pulled him away. It was the store bouncer. If he'd been there at the start, maybe none of this would've happened. But then if I'd gone into the store a few minutes later, or if the second counter had stayed open, or if the bouncer had stayed in the stockroom... Schrödinger, and his cat, have never been more relevant. You only know what's going to happen when you see it happen. Sorry. I'm digressing. I've got a lot of time for digressions now.

You see — my angry unprovoked assailant? He was dead.

*

At the trial, I expected the track-suited fellow to back me up, but he didn't see it my way at all. "I've known big Ivan for years," he said. "We wis just joshin. Ay? Friendly. Ay? But this guy here?" He pointed at me. "Hittin a disabled pensioner. Shockin, man. Shockin. Knew exactly whit he was doin, like. Just took him out." Yes, the disability thing didn't help my case. Given how well he was throwing those punches, how was I supposed to know he was registered disabled?

The bouncer? Turns out he 'saw nothing'. The counter assistant who'd been serving big Ivan? He'd 'gone to get the bouncer'. The other witnesses? Long gone by the time the police arrived, at speed — as you might expect from the coves who frequent Money Merchants.

'Culpable homicide', the prosecutor said, and the jury believed her. The judge was 'unimpressed' by what she called my 'elaborate fakery'. That hurt me as much as the conviction. I'm a scientist, for God's sake.

41

*

I got six years, but my lawyer said I should be out in three. That's not as bad as it sounds. The vicarious social observation may keep me amused, if I can avoid the unwelcome attention of the more thuggish, or hyper-sexualised, of my co-residents. So I'm definitely planning to keep my eyes down, my mouth shut and, following the advice my good lady frequently used to offer me, to 'keep that smile' off my 'supercilious face'.

Oh, and another thing: that one punch — impressively delivered as it undoubtedly was — will be the one and only demonstration of my skills in the pugilistic art. It may have been my first... But, I can assure you, it will also be my last.

James Andrew

Self-Portrait with Pen

I am a man with a pen,
and I grasp at life with it.

The journey of sunlight through a room,
the tread of a foot on grass,
the sound of a bird winging into day:

my glance at the world is often hesitant
but my hunger for the moment
is so great I will not let it go

but make the minute dance
on the point of my pen.

Steve O'Brien

The Summer Ball

Susan Harris,
bathed in summer fragrance
stands all alone on platform 1.
Her father in the car park
smiles, thumbs up,
can't stop the pounding of her heart.

On tiptoes and
with trembling hands,
she shades her eyes
from the dying sun;
till squealing and hissing
through steam kissed air
the train arrives.

After a moment,
doors burst open,
strewing passengers
happily homeward;
at the rear,
the guard steps down
to take his place
behind the crowd.

Till finally, the last door slams;
like a shotgun blast
to strike her heart.
A whistle blows,
the train moves on,
and Susan Harris,
bathed in summer fragrance
stands all alone on platform 1.

Soup of the Day

She looked at him as he put the apron on.

"Do you want to wear that?" she asked.

"I don't want to splash my golf club sweater," he said. "Or my golfing slacks."

She looked at his noisy trousers and thought you'd be hard pressed to see a stain on that pattern. "The first thing we need to do is make a stock."

"Aye, well how do we make that?" he asked as if she should know what he didn't know. And she did know what he didn't know. "Mind I've got to be on the tee at twelve o'clock."

"And it's time you learned to make soup."

"I know," he said.

"I mean what age are you and you can't make soup?"

"Well, I never had time."

"Well, you've time now. Go and get me the ham hough out of the fridge."

He presented her with the ham hough wrapped in plastic.

"For God's sake, take it out the packing."

She watched him struggle and his face redden and after a few minutes he looked at her and she saw the small puzzled boy inside the angry old man. "Why do they have to wrap everything so you can't get it out?"

She handed him the kitchen scissors and he produced the piece of meat, bone and skin and handed it to her. Then he bent down and picked up the hacked pieces of plastic that lay on the kitchen floor.

"What did you do before you retired?" she asked sarcastically.

"You know I was in sales."

"I see," she said. "See this ham?"

"Yes, I see the ham. I can see that ham. Of course, I can see that ham."

"That is a smoked ham."

"A smoked ham, yea."

"Now, you need to rinse this a couple times in the pan because it will be too salty."

"Can you get an unsmoked one?" he asked, being smart.

"You can but you'll find that the flavour is not as deep. So you are better to get a smoked ham but you will have to rinse it." Christ, this is going to be a long day, she thought.

"But if I got an unsmoked ham I wouldn't have to rinse it?"

"But the soup wouldn't taste as nice," she said as she gritted her teeth. "Now get the big pan."

"Which pan is the big pan?"

"The big pan is the big pan," she said.

He looked round the tops of the units and then round the walls.

"It's in the cupboard under the cooker."

He went to the cupboard and found the pan. "Would it not be better if you got the pan out before you started? You could get everything out that you need and like assemble the tools on the worktop before you start so that you've got all your tools ready for use."

It was her turn to look at the walls. "How many times in our thirty-nine years together have you made soup?"

He thought for a moment. "Never."

"Put the ham in the fuckin' pan and walk over to the sink, that's the big stainless steel unit against the wall with the hot-cold taps, and rinse the ham twice in cold water."

He glumly followed her instructions, swirling the ham under the cold tap. He turned the tap on at full throttle, soaking the apron and the kitchen floor. She went to the cupboard, took out the mop and cleaned up after him.

"I think I rinsed it three times. Is that okay, dear?"

"Yes, that's okay."

"But I wouldn't have to do that if I bought an unsmoked ham?"

"Never mind the unsmoked ham. Now fill the pan to about three quarters with cold water and put it on the gas."

He managed this.

"Now get an onion and a carrot and cut the carrot into chunks and cut the onion in half."

He went to the cutlery drawer and took out a knife and started to hack away at the carrot.

"That's a butter knife. Get the big knife."

"There wasn't a big knife there."

"It's in the drawer next to the cutlery drawer where I keep the vegetable and carving knives."

"Would it not be a good idea to keep all the knives in the cutlery drawer so you've got everything together?"

"Just get the big knife and keep it away from me. And get the chopping board and don't cut anything directly on my worktops."

"The chopping board, is that yon white thing?"

"Yes, indeed it is," she said.

He got the big knife and the chopping board and managed to cut the carrot into chunks.

"Now cut the onion in half."

"With the big knife on the chopping board?"

"Yes, with the big knife on the chopping board."

After he had done that he looked at her.

"Put them in the pan."

He put them in the pan.

"I've put them in the pan," he said.

"I see that. You'll have noticed that there is some parsley on the worktop."

"That green stuff."

"Yes that green stuff. Now tear off the stalks and put them in the pan with the carrot and onion."

"And the ham. You cannae forget the ham."

"Indeed you cannot forget the ham."

"Why just the stalks?"

"Because you'll chop the tops up at the end to add to the soup. It'll give the soup a bit of colour so that it'll look better and give it a bit more taste."

"Why can't I just throw in the lot? It would be easier."

"Just do it."

He gave her a look and then tore the stalks from the leaves of the parsley.

"Throw them in the pan."

He gathered up the stalks and threw them in the pan. "I just thought it would be easier..."

"For God's sake, how long have I been making the soup for this house?"

"Yea, all right."

"Now, get the pepper grinder, take the top off and take out eight or ten peppercorns."

"Which is it?"

"Which is what?"

"Is it eight or ten peppercorns?"

"Either."

"Should you not be precise?"

"Nine, get nine peppercorns and put them in the pan."

He painstakingly took the top off the grinder and counted out nine peppercorns onto the worktop and scooped them up and dropped them into the pan.

"See how easy that was," she said in those strained tones that you use when you've been taken to the outer edges of your sanity. "Now turn up the gas and bring it to the boil."

47

"And then what?"

"Once it's boiling, turn down that gas so that it simmers for maybe a couple of hours."

"And that's you made soup?" he smiled.

"No, that's you made the stock."

"Aw, Jesus Christ, can we no' just open a tin?"

"No, you've got to do this properly. When I'm gone I don't want you reaching for the frying pan or the tin opener."

He dropped his head and when he brought it up his eyes were full of tears.

"I'll never learn all that," he said. "Not without you."

"Don't worry, the consultant said I should have three good months. That should be long enough."

"I don't think I can handle this," he said. "I'm no' strong like you."

"You'll be all right, pet. I'll show you." She walked over to him and pulled him to her. His head fell on her shoulder.

"Did you get the butcher meat?" she asked.

He nodded, words being beyond him.

She put her fingers under his chin and lifted his head and she looked him in the eye and said:

"Tomorrow, I'll show you how to make your favourite stew."

A C Clarke

Alive

The goat becomes a shout
the children gasp at

as it charges
a hill cropped

by oblivious sheep.
Is it in pain,

an unborn kid twisting
its belly?

Has it gulped a stash
of deathcap?

Surely it cries a fierce
affirmative:

of summer grass
of salt-sharp air

that flows into its joyous lungs
while every bound

removes it further from
the greying sands

where a beached carcase
gapes, ribs snapped,

heart ripped out,
unable to outstrip

the running sea,
echo the wind's shriek

in the thunder of its
long-since-tattered sails.

Seth Crook

Swimming Apart, Together

We meet at the beach
but keep two metres apart:

when changing
        when drying
when walking in
        when swimming
when singing.

Curious young seals
not yet so wary of our species
swim close to us.
And no tourists sing.
Few will arrive this year.
So the bay belongs to us
and the kilroys of the surface:

when circling the buoy
        when swimming through the wrack
when bathing in the sun
        when swimming with the tide.

At times we are closer to them
than we are each other.
We can touch the seals
but not each other.

Jean Rafferty

When the Snows Came

When the snows came
I did not think of the plum tree in my garden
nor the thick stone walls of our home.
I do not look back.

This is my home.
We live next to a man driven mad by loss.
Tents stretch in grey ranks to the horizon,
misery multiplied.

When the snows came
mud swirled up like weird rock forms.
There was no wood left to make a fire.
I was afraid we'd die in the night.

My son ran barefoot
in the snow. He's only little.
His foot should be soft but is rough as wood.
I hate to touch it.

I do not look back.
I would like my mother's silver coffee pot,
not these battered old pans.
I miss our battered old stove.

But mostly I wish
my son would stop growing
so the food they give me
is enough to feed him.

And oh, I want my husband.

Taste

On the snow-flecked journey to the edge of town I had no high expectations. Being told in advance that you're going to be amazed inevitably results in disappointment. I had no reason to think otherwise this time. Brick told me I'd be impressed visiting the grave of his recently-deceased grandparents — an odd thing to say, not to mention an odd thing to do late on Christmas Eve. He assured me the sight would astound me, the first of its kind he told me, and really expensive. As we passed through the gated entrance he was excited. I was cold.

Okay Brick, where is it? I asked.

It's at the other end of the cemetery, Cammy, a kind of private area where the lairs cost a whole lot more and there's security cameras an' all that.

Aye, of course it would be at the expensive end, I thought.

In recent years Brick's family had become rather fascinated with money and what it can buy. Following the discovery of a new kind of synthetic quick-build construction material the family business had multiplied its profits. From working class roots his dad had experienced a sudden rise to wealth. Just moved into a brand new five bed detached villa in the area known locally as Millionaires Row. They filled it with expensive but tasteless furniture, giant TVs, electronic devices, glass and metal objects adorned with bling and crystal. Mercedes and Porsche in the garage, all the over-the-top essential non-essentials.

Now I should make it clear that Brick is my pal whom I love dearly and I really don't envy his parents' good fortune. But I never felt at home in their new property. On the other hand I had had the pleasure of visiting his grandparents a couple of times and felt more at home with them. It seems they were never entirely comfortable with the trappings of wealth and had remained unchanged by their son's newfound riches. To them nouveau riche just sounded like nouvelle cuisine, something that was not to their taste; they liked filled plates of plain and wholesome food. They were hospitable by nature, forcing cups of tea and toasted scones upon anyone who visited. When their son offered to build them a little bungalow on his land they refused to move from their two bedroom council tenancy.

The story of their deaths I remember had a simple poetry about it. Both in their eighties, his grandma continued to look after grandpa to the end. He had been in bed calling for a cup of tea when he sustained a massive heart attack.

Grandma accompanied Brick's dad to the hospital but the medics there were unable to save him. As the doctor confirmed his demise grandma called out his name then, unable to let him go on alone, succumbed to a fatal stroke and joined him.

As the light snow turned to chilly wet sleet, we made our way to the furthest corner of the cemetery where Brick glanced back at me with a smile, then looked around quickly in the darkness as if checking that no one else was watching. He pulled a remote control from his designer hoodie, whispering, *Watch how cool this is*, directed the device and pressed a button. As my eyes adjusted to the darkness I saw that there was a low building ahead of us and a door on it was opening slowly, a pale light spilling from inside. He signalled for me to follow him in.

There it was in all its glory. A grave much as you'd see anywhere but on a larger scale, surrounded by a chunky black marble border, its oversized white marble headstone inscribed with rose gold lettering. I didn't get round to reading the inscription however, because my eye was drawn to the animated green hologram in front of it. Distracted, I could think only of that wee hologram of Princess Leia in the first Star Wars movie I saw.

What ya thinkin'? Brick asked, but I couldn't tell him I was thinking about how money can't buy taste.

Anyway I quickly dismissed that thought when I saw what the holographic performance depicted. Brick's grandpa seated in a chair, his standing grandma on gif-style repeat pouring for eternity from a never-emptying teapot into the never-filled mug held by her husband. It finishes with them both smiling outward and waving to visitors.

"What you thinking mate?" Brick repeated. "Be honest man."

"I'm thinkin' perfect, mate. Perfect."

Dai Vaughan

The March

The pipes and drums resound
as they walk down into the city centre
The boom of the bass drum
The rattle of drumsticks
The shrill sound of the silver flutes
This is no empty parade
This is belief
Don't mess with us

Peter Russell

The Post Great War Rag

Let's all do the post Great War Rag,
Along with impersonators wearing drag
Last year we were in the mud-filled trenches
Now we're sitting on the cheap seat benches
We've left the war in Flanders and France
And we want to see the showgirls dance
We're throwing a peace to end in pieces ball
At the hollow Victory music hall

Do that crazy Rag, post crazy Great War
Getting what we thought we fought for
This time last year we were all in hell
Today it's only peanuts getting shelled
Now we don't shoot, we laugh and clap
We've wiped Kaiser Bill's huns off the map
The glare is limelight not Very light bursts
When we see the girls lift up their skirts

Do that Rag, post a War called Great
With new ethnic nations to create
Down the Hall of Mirrors at Versailles
Stare the ghosts of our mates who died
For Johnny Turk and Jerry it's humiliation
From Sykes-Picot and reparations
It's the Big Three's own slapstick show:
Lloyd George, Wilson and Clemenceau

We lucky ones who saw the whole show through
Have a new big killer — pandemic flu
We don't need gas and guns for slaughter
That Spanish virus brings mortality in short order
So if we have any remaining close relations
We'll pawn our medals for their cremations
Let's pack up our shellshock in our old kitbag
Doing that great post Great War Rag

55

Meg Gannon

The Moon

The moon invaded my dreams,
cast its light through the window,
spreading slowly across the floor
to find its reach.

Then, wide-eyed, it faced me,
held me in its beam as I stood
transfixed.

I looked away, around the walls
and into the corners of the room,
anywhere bar the face of the moon,
and I asked the stars to follow,
falling one at a time.

But the moon alone
decided to release me,
cast off its ropes and sailed
slowly traversing the sky,
leaving only shadows
clinging like ivy to the walls.

When the Stars Fell

I remember when the stars fell
under your spell
onto my tongue,
my skin,
my bones,
sinking deep into my soul
where they will
always
always
burn like gold.

Federation of Writers (Scotland)
2020 Vernal Equinox Competition

Prizewinners

Gaelic:
1 Seonaidh Adams
2 Eòghan Stiùbhart
3 Niall O'Gallagher

Flash Fiction:
1 Ruth Gilchrist
2 Mary Edward
3 Wendy Jones

Scots:
1 Donald Adamson
2 Fran Baillie
3 Lynn Valentine

Poetry:
1 Roger Elkin
2 Stephen Keeler
3 Mark Vernon Thomas

Short Story:
1 Rachel Carmichael
2 Kirsten MacQuarrie
3 Shirley Gillan

Judges:

Gaelic:	Màiri Anna NicUalraig
Flash fiction:	Stephen Barnaby
Scots:	Sheila Templeton
Poetry:	Finola Scott
Short stories:	Charlie Gracie

Seonaidh Adams

An Crogan

Uair, bha aig na diathan crogan òir agus chùm iad aca fhèin sna sgòthan e. Bha e dealrach is glòrmhor. Dhèanadh muinntir ghlas an t-saoghail fodhpa ùrnaigh ach am faigheadh iad cuid de na bha am broinn a' chrogain gus loinn a chur air na beathannan glas' aca. An-dràsta sa-rithist agus nam biodh fonn fialaidh orra, nochdadh aon de na diathan an crogan dha na daoine mar shealladh air nach robh aca.

Chòrdadh an tighearnas seo ri na diathan agus mar bu bhitheanta bha iad eudmhor, sanntach agus air am beò-ghlacadh len ìomhaigh fhèin.

Ach latha de na laithean, dh'èirich aimhreit eadar na diathan. Air adhbhar air choireigin, dh'èirich an droch nàdar is chaidh iad an amhaich a-chèile. Chualas an tàirneanaich shìos am measg an t-sloigh iomagainich. Chaidh na speuran an sracadh le gathan dealanaich. San onghail, cha tugadh feart air a' chrogan.

Thuit e.

Chan e rathad furasta a bha aige is e a' tuiteam tro na sgothan is speuran.

Chaidh a shiabadh le na gaothan uile is miann aig gach tè aca air an t-saidhbhreas seo. Chaidh a shlacadh leis an dìle-bhàite, sneachda is clachan-meallain. Agus fad an t-siubhail, gathan na grèine ga sholasachadh am fianais a' chinne-daonna.

Cha robh nì air thalamh a sheasadh ri dochann mar sin. Ged a thuit an crogan bhon iarmailt, cha do ràinig e an talamh. Chaidh e à sealladh ach chunnacas, na àite, bogha de dhiofar dhathan a' sìneadh eadar an t-adhar agus am fearann.

An-toiseach, sheas na daoine an làrach nam bonn a' coimhead air an ìongnadh ioma-dhathach seo sìnte os an cionn agus tarsainn nam beann. Ach rè ùine, ruith iad ga ionnsaigh is toileachas nan ceumannan cabhagach. Airson a' chiad uair, chaidh na diathan greannach air dìochuimhn' orra.

Mar a thachair, cha robh agus chan eil crogan òir aig ceann a' bhogha-froise. Se an t-òr.

Glossary:

air dìochuimhn' — *forgotten*
aimhreit — *discord, trouble*
an làrach nam bonn — *on the spot*
chaidh a shlacadh — *it was thrashed*
chaidh a shiabadh — *it was buffeted*
chaidh iad an amhaich a-chèile — *they fought amongst each other*
cha tugadh feart air a' chrogan — *no-one paid attention to the crock*
dochann — *beating, punishment*
fonn fialaidh — *feeling generous*
loinn a chur — *to brighten up*
mar a thachair — *as it turned out*
tighearnas — *lordship*

Gaelic Category First Prize

Peallag

Shìos ris an abhainn
chunnaic mi an-dè i
Peallag bhochd
le leadan salach
coltas a' phris air
ceann gun chìreadh
's i gun mhothachadh
air steall an earraich
a' ruith seachad oirre
's i a' brunndail rithe fèin

Nan robh an sruth na sgàthan
cha dhèanadh i càil dheth
's coma leatha an saoghal
's coma leis an t-saoghal i
aonragan truagh
am meadhan a' bhaile
na daoine sìthe
cuide rinn fhathast
ach 's sinne nach eil
airson am faicinn.

English translation

Down by the river I saw the other day poor Peallag* with her filthy tresses, looking like she'd been dragged through a bush, bonce uncombed and unaware of the spring spate rushing past her, grunting and mumbling to herself.

If the stream were a mirror, it would be of no use to her, she doesn't care for the world, or the world for her, a pitiful solitary in the middle of the city; the faeries, the quiet ones, they are with us still, it's just we don't want to see them.

*Peallag is a Highland solitary, who could be found next to lochans and rivers, sitting with her unkempt hair covering her face, never once combing or tending to it, and although she was always next to the water she would never look at her own reflection. Peallag can also mean a rough garment or hairy skin. The spirit had several variations on the name, Pealltach, Pealltag, and most notably Peallaidh, from which we get Obar Pheallaidh/Aberfeldy/The Confluence of the Peallaidh River in Perthshire.

Gaelic Category Second Prize

Niall O'Gallagher

Caisearbhan

'S ionmhainn leam an caisearbhan
 le falt na gile maoithe
gèilleadh ris a' chagaran,
 rosadh le anail ghaoithe.
Sìl dannsadh gu h-aighearach,
 air bàrr an aiteil aoibhinn,
cur nan car le caisreabhachd
 oiteige graide faoine.

Gaelic Category Third Prize

Nereid

Spring — Limassol
From his usual seat outside Twin's taverna, opposite the cathedral Ayia Napa, he catches sight of her. He can tell she has been here long enough to learn to walk on the shadowed side of the street, but not long enough to slow her steps. Leaving a handful of small coins on the table Vasilis gets up. He will follow her, at least a little way, she is not his, not yet, but he is concerned she will lose herself in these tangled streets, and he is more than a little curious.

Autumn — Limassol
He will leave the city soon, return to his hillside village, back to the peaches and nectarines, the olives and grapes, back for the harvest. Tonight, he leaves his friends to their game of Tavla and wanders through the park. He sees her beneath the flame tree, waiting for him on their bench. He steps lighter now towards her, ready to call her name — she turns, it is not her face. The hand that rises to wave is adrift for a moment, he stumbles then steadies himself against the smooth bark of a eucalyptus. Back in the summer she had crushed the seed kernels between her fingers, holding her hands to his face so he could inhale the soothing aroma.

The next day his skin feels the breeze coming in off the sea, he knows there is little time left, he must leave soon. Before he prepares, he takes coffee at her favourite café, the one beside the castle, the one that serves omelettes large enough to share. And there approaching is the sway of her walk, the cut of her skirt, he wills the wind to whip it above her knees. She has stopped, she is talking to someone, laughing, it is not her voice, it is not her.

His last evening, he sits at the open window, he chuckles at sparrows squabbling in the dust.

His mind turns, to begin closing the shutters, and she is there, before the stove, smiling at him. He rises to greet her but here is his neighbour calling through the window, "Vasilis, be sure and take your cat with you, we've enough of them here." When he turns again to his love — she has left the room.

In the morning the clouds are building in the south but, before departing, he goes down to the sea for one last morning swim. He wants to wash the dust of this city away. Of course, she has made it there before him, already she is far out, beyond the breakwater.

Flash Fiction First Prize

Mary Edward

As Good As New

It's raining on the gnome. Elsie wipes a small space on the misted window to look out into the gardens. Behind her the ward is filled with the chatter of visitors, but she doesn't have any. Instead she looks at the gnome.

It sits buried up to its bottom in a muddy flower bed. Since she came in with her broken hip she's asked everyone — nurses, doctors, auxiliaries — how a garden gnome found its way to a hospital. No-one knows. So Elsie decides that someone put it there to cheer up a patient. It must have been a long time ago, because the gnome has lost its colour. Stuck there in all weathers, until the plastic has become bone-white and almost transparent. She wonders for a frightening moment if the gnome is a ghost, maybe sent by Walter to haunt her.

The thought makes her shiver and she eases herself on to the bed and pulls the cover over her.

Walter had always hated her garden gnomes, but she'd never given in on that one, continuing to add to her little dwarf family until they were the first thing anyone noticed when they came in the gate. He said they were ridiculous, but Elsie loved them all, with their smiling faces which never changed.

When they got a bit unkempt in the winter — Walter drew the line at sheltering them in the house — she'd sneak them into the kitchen one by one while he was at work and freshen up their paint, until their eyes twinkled at her again. Walter would sniff loudly at the smell of acetate, and shake his head.

The ward is quiet. The visitors have gone. Elsie struggles out of bed for another look at the gnome. The light shining out of the window makes a cold veil of the falling rain. It runs over the gnome's blind eyes and drips from the end of its nose. The sight pains her.

The pain bores deeper when she remembers the skip and her gnomes being tossed into it by the men who cleared her house. Her son had arranged it all from New York. Walter was dead and the house was too big. The good furniture to auction, the rubbish to the dump and Elsie to sheltered housing.

In the morning the doctor comes to tell her it's time to leave. Her hip replacement has been a success and an ambulance will take her home after lunch. She's as good as new, he says. She doesn't know whether to laugh or cry.

It has stopped raining and the gnome is drying out, but there are green streaks on its face, like tears.

When they come for her she whispers to the paramedics as they push her out into the grounds. And the ambulance doors close on Elsie and the gnome, tucked inside the blanket over her knees.

Tomorrow she will give the home-help some money to buy paint.

Flash Fiction Second Prize

Sod off, Hilary

She nods at you, this colleague of yours, whose name you've forgotten.

"Journey okay, Sal?"

"Fine thanks."

What journey? You're in the office. You got here somehow. It must have been fine.

"Lucky you," she says. "My train was a nightmare. Squashed like pilchards, we were."

You smile at her. Pilchards. You haven't got a clue what she's going on about. You mean that literally. You really don't know. What. She. Is... The sentence is gone.

You log on. A miracle. Yesterday you just stared at the screen as if you were waiting for it to give you instructions. You saw a number for the IT helpdesk on the wall. You called it and said your computer wasn't working and one of them, not the good-looking one, the other one, was there in minutes and fiddled around and said there didn't seem to be a problem now. You thanked him and said computers have a mind of their own. And he made a joke about AI, which you didn't really get. Funny how every day's different. How can you remember what happened yesterday but this morning you don't know how you got to work? It must have been by bus. It's usually by bus, isn't it?

You need help. You know you need help.

She hovers by your desk, looking as if she wants to chat.

"What did you think of Tom's email about the new pharmaceutical account?"

What email? You get lots of emails. Bluff it. And what is her name?

"Yes, interesting," you say. Was that the wrong thing to say? She stares at you, and you wish she wouldn't. What is this thing, this random nothingness? Sometimes you wake up and you don't know where you are or why, like waking up in a hotel room and for a moment you can't work out your surroundings. Except you're at home, in the bed you've slept in for twenty years. Other times, it's okay first thing, you feel quite sharp, but then it happens, someone's snipping away with wire-cutters in your brain. Or the slugs get in, secreting something thick and sticky that clogs up the machinery.

You always had a way with images. Making concepts concrete. But what if ideas dry up? Or worse, words go? Words are your sustenance. Without them, there's nothing, you're finished.

You need help. You need to talk to someone.

She's still staring, but crinkling her eyes, as if she's trying to smile with them. She's pitying you, goddamn her. "Look, Sal, I don't know how to say this, but are you okay? You seem, well, a bit spaced out at times. If you want to talk..."

Hilary — that's her name. She's a friend, but why would you want to talk? Stop interfering, you should tell her. Sod off, Hilary.

"No, everything's fine, thanks."

She turns away and you look at your screen. There's work to do. You cross your fingers and concentrate hard and hope.

Flash Fiction Third Prize

Donald Adamson

The Sun Athort the Lift

The day A hae a notion tae retour
tae the strand we wan tae ilka year
for oor Sunday Schuil trip
on Carruthers' auld glaur-broun-and-reid
gear-crinchin diesel-smeekin bus
whase climb frae New Abbey tae Colvend gied us
oor first sicht o the sea that we hailsed
wi cheerin and pyntin
ayewis at yon same lang streetch o shore perfectit
for moat-and-castle-biggin and for splashin
aa efternuin till wi the tide's ebbin
and the day's dwynin cam the gaitherin up
o buckets and spades and the wabbit traik
in unshuik-oot-shuin and shell-grittit
breeks and sarks tae the bus for oor jurney hame
throu Dalbeattie-o-the-causeyed-streets
as Sulwath watters stertit on their ain
simmer-nicht-lang surge tae America
for anither dawin, anither muivin-o-the-sun
athort the lift, ither bairns
playin on the saund.

Scots Category First Prize

Fran Baillie

Coast Lines

They cah ye East Neuk, thon coarner o the Kingdom that turns its heid awa
fae the jahs o the michty Forth tae faiss the North Sea,
slappit wi its gurlie storms, smoort beh yon smirry haar, kisst beh its slack watter.
Gulls scythe the skehs, seaburd sabres owre spindrift,
dank air gasht as they mew an wheel.

Yer features mark ye oot.
Yer stubblt baird fae Elie tae St Monans,
Ainster's harbourt mooth,
yer prood neb at the Ness abin Crail,
thon runklie broo an sandy fringe o Cambo.

James, oor reid-heidit Sixth, spake thae words o ye, 'a beggar's mantle fringed with gold'.
Were his thochts then o yer frayed rocky shores an sandglister
or did he see the labours o yer puir fisherfowk tae bring hame the riches o the sea,
the silver darlins, russet partans an the saut fae its brine?
Mibbie he hid in mind thon treasures that flowed in fae the Low Countries,
wines, silks, and Flemish websters wi thir fine woven cloths fit fir a king's claes?

Yet midst thon muckle trade in Holland's gowden age
nae Dutch maisters cam tae bide, tae convey yer countenance wi iles an canvas.
But noo, Scotland's ain hae flockit tae mak thir hame in yer neuks an crannies,
drahn beh yir shimmerin licht an cheengin hues,
tae plant thir easels, ply thir alchemy, frame yer harbours an yer coves,
rouge yer pantiled ruifs an gray yer crah-steppit gables, aa tae capture yer abidin smile.

Scots Category Second Prize

Lynn Valentine

Munlochy

We knottit oor wishes roon the well,
tyit them a' tae the trees, white fir a bairn,
blue fir a cuir. Wir nervish gaggles
ringin at corbies croakin' in the auld oaks.
Nane grantit, nane lastit, the reid
runnin', the blackness takin' ower
us baith. You awa by simmerdim,
me an ma belly emptie.
Noo they're clearin' the woods,
takin' awa the sheets, the cloots,
even a pair o drawers.
A think the last wid mak ye laugh.
A wish a could still ca ye Mither,
see yir heid turn roon at ma call.
Some grey efternuins I dauner,
echo yir name in tae the well.

Scots Category Third Prize

Roger Elkin

Remembering Vukovar

Bundled from hospital beds, they came
as they stood — or rather lay. Most of them.
So getting them shifted to feet was difficult.
Had to be prodded and shoved — the shouting,
the kicking. The groans, screams. The stink

of wounds, of rotting limbs. So came, atlases
of suffering mapped blood-brown on bandages
and slings. Came with nothing. Just the clothes
they wore — torn, dirt-smudged, bullet-singed;
their shoes with soles flapping. No luggage.

Came first to barracks, then bussed to the farm's
dead-end hangar, its walls-tall steel sheeting,
grey and faceless and wider than a tractor, and
impenetrable but for the sliding personnel door,
through which were hustled, one by one, to face

chains, clubs, baseball bats, rifle stocks, sticks.
Four of them — Kemo, Damjan, Zeljko, Siniša —
killed right there; the rest stripped of pocketed
belongings, so where they stood, or cowered
in fear, were kerchiefs, spectacles, loose notes,

change, more change, the paper waste of ID cards,
wallets, purses — all the tranklements of being,
scattered on the splattered hangar floor proclaiming
"This is me", "Is what I am", "Is mine, all mine".
And stayed so until sundown. Then, around six o'clock,

were split into groups of ten to twenty, and trucked
the bumpy ride to the wooded ravine, two hundred
yards away. The enfilade ready with raised AK-47s.
The bulldozer nudging at the mass grave edge.
By ten that night all two hundred and sixty-one had been killed.

No need, then, for the stuff of living, its niceties:
Food   water   to drink   to wash.
No soap   no towel   no toothbrush.
Just the taste of fear,
the wet of blood, the smell of death.

Poetry First Prize

Stephen Keeler

Snow Moon

To the west, a vast
end-of-the-world skybrow;

from the east, nothing
to intimate anything again.

Mediating both, the snow moon —
crumbling pale cake

a child might nibble
curled up under lamplight

with a book, looking
through the blizzard

while the house is trying
to get back to sleep.

Poetry Second Prize

Mark Vernon Thomas

With the Accent on Place

with reference to '*In My Country*' by Jackie Kay

I try and roll my vowels like tyres
but they stay flat.

Not the flat of northern folk
from fells and dales, mills and moors
still re-running the war of the roses.

No: mine are the sounds of the south,
deep-south overseas, deep sheep country,
with bleets and baahs and close-cropped syllables,

not an aar in sight: no burrs,
just biddy bids — less pronounced,
no less prickly for a' that.

In Scottish bays and braes
I stick out, a Kiwi at a ceilidh;
and when the questions come,

inexorable as erosion, the answer —
these paats mate, these paats —
doesn't hold back the tide.

I don't pass for a local:
but local I am —
this is my place too,

my turangawaewae, here
in the west.
Home now,

with gannet seas and
the guard-dog baakks of deer at dusk
an echo

of long-ago.

Biddy bids: *the NZ burr, an Acaena species. From the Maori:* piripiri – *sticky, prickly, annoying!*
Turangawaewae: *the standing place, our place in the world*

Poetry Third Prize

God's Amazing Grace

Now I've even lost Sunday afternoons. One hour to myself but nowhere to enjoy a coffee. The maths tutor directs me to the Asda near her house.

There's a row of smaller shops close to the supermarket. Bookies, takeaway, a post office. A few men are setting something up in front of the Chicken Palace. They have banners and a speaker. One of them wears an old-fashioned hat — a trilby or a fedora, I'm not sure — and is saying one-two one-two into a microphone.

A metal shutter is pulled down over the front of the Chicken Palace and someone has spray painted the word SEX in huge capital letters on it. The men look serious, most of them smartly dressed in suits with anoraks on top. One has close-cropped hair and is wearing a heavy jumper, ribbed with patches on the shoulders, army style. They notice me looking at them. The one in the hat waves to me, beckons and points to where some other people are waiting. The audience, I guess.

I point to my watch and give him a smile and keep walking into the supermarket.

I'm looking for the wholewheat penne when someone starts to speak to me. His appearance distracts me from what he's saying. He has a long blond ponytail but his hair at the front is short, and greasy grey curls are sticking to his forehead.

Sorry what was that? I say.

He nods to a packet of king prawns in his trolley and holds up two jars of pasta sauce.

I'm cooking dinner tonight, he says. What sauce goes with prawns?

He looks pleased about something. I guess that he's cooking for a woman and that this is not an event that occurs often.

Not the cheese, I say to him. Not with prawns. The tomato would be better.

Not the cheese? he says.

Even just some olive oil with garlic and chilli. Or chilli flakes, less effort.

I leave it at that and push my trolley to the next aisle, his patchouli and body odour still with me. I've not picked up any pasta. I worry about what kind of arse goes on about olive oil and chilli flakes to someone who looks like he lives off microwaves and the chippy, then I feel bad about being prejudiced. I decide that I did the right thing, I said what I would say to anyone who asked me what to do with prawns, and he won't take my advice anyway; he just wants people to know about his date.

Ellie will be starving after an hour of maths so I go to the biscuits and crisps. I'm studying the snacks, wondering whether I have the energy to insist on fruit, when the prawn guy appears again, holding up a bag of crisps.

Check this out, he says. He points to the list of ingredients and taps his fingers on the words. Suitable for vegetarians, he says.

That's good.

No, look. He turns over the packet, taps. Roast chicken flavour. Chicken.

I try to look astounded.

He puts the packet that he's tapped and handled back on the shelf. I'm stuck in some irresistible magnetic trolley orbit with him. I'm going to see him in every aisle and he'll look at me and I'll have to nod and smile and he'll keep showing me things.

I go to the checkout and pay for my stuff then dump it all in the food bank basket, other than the Sunday paper. I watch out for him. Twice he's spoken to me. Either I look like a serious foodie or he thinks he's on a roll now he's persuaded one woman to come round for dinner. On my way out I get a cup of tea to go.

Back in the car, doors locked, the window slightly open so the tea doesn't steam it up. I tuck my nose into my scarf — inhale Mitsouko to remind me that there is beauty in this world — and I unfold the newspaper. I have the best two minutes of my weekend before a knock at the window. It's the military jumper man, making a circular movement with his finger.

I respond to the authority of his knitwear, but only by a couple of centimetres. His mouth is right in the gap — teeth somehow better than I expect — and he says, if you've got some time to kill would you mind holding my mum's brolly for a while? It's my brother preaching today.

He indicates a woman in a wheelchair up at the Chicken Palace. The guy in the hat is with her.

I can't, I'm sorry, I say. I have to leave at ten to.

That's okay. My sister'll be here in a few minutes. Bring your tea.

I follow him. There's a congregation of five.

Mum, this nice lady is going to look after you till Yvonne gets here, he says. The mum looks at me.

She wanny us? she says to him.

I try to think of a good reason to leave.

83

Behave yourself, Mum. You'll have to watch out for her, she's fulla nonsense.

Thanks very much, dear, the old woman says.

I put my tea down somewhere I think I won't kick it over and hold a big umbrella over the two of us. Her chair is in a large puddle I can't avoid standing in if I'm to keep the rain off her.

She looks over the side of her chair at my light grey boots.

You should always waterproof your suede, she says.

The man in the hat has the microphone in his hand. His brother stands beside him, hands clasped in front, eyes scanning the car park — for signs of trouble, I imagine.

Welcome, friends. Join us as we worship the Lord on His day. On this His day. Let us share in the wonder of God's amazing grace.

He reads from the bible. The old woman pulls at my sleeve, quite hard. I have to bend down towards her.

That's an unfortunate backdrop they've got today, she says. She points at the graffiti on the metal shutter behind her son and starts to rock her shoulders forward and back, her mouth stretched over her teeth and her face contorted in an exaggerated silent laugh.

It is quite funny, isn't it, I say.

Her son's voice booms out.

Who. So. Ever.

Shall not perish.

But shall have.

Everlasting life.

Whosoever, friends.

His mother pulls my sleeve and she's off again, with the rocking and the face. She tries to point to something behind him but she can't keep her finger straight. A rat is crawling out from a gap at the bottom of the Chicken Palace's metal shutter. It sits behind the preacher son, its head up, attentive, while his mother heaves and pulls faces. For a second the rat and I lock eyes.

I'm dying to drink my tea, but the rain has been falling into it and I think about what the raindrops might have collected on their way down from the clouds, the pollution and the dirt and the exhaust fumes and the exhalations and evaporations. The emanations of people and rats.

Haw, a voice says.

It's the prawn guy, out on the loose in the car park, walking towards me. He looks as menacing as anyone can with hair like that and an Asda carrier in each hand.

Are you wanny them?

I look at the old woman but her eyes are closed in prayer now and there's feedback from the speaker. Anyway, I don't feel inclined to explain myself.

You can stick your garlic and your chilli, he says.

I wonder what he might do if he didn't have his hands full. He walks away.

I curse my eagerness to please and my devoted parents and the stupid good girl that they made me. And exams and tutors and complex numbers.

The old woman opens her eyes and looks at me.

You're not scared of a wee rat are you? she says.

Short Story First Prize

Kirsten MacQuarrie
The Wordsworth Women

The wedding ring does not fit. All night, I felt it slipping around my thin-boned finger, a spun gold celestial that refused to stay fixed in place unless I curled my hand into a fist. My joints, at least, are thicker and almost bulbous: knuckles swollen from scrubbing over well-worn kitchen boards or from laying down seeds into slumbering earth that already holds the chill of winter.

Restless, I watched as the ring's reflected shadows loomed and leered at me through the darkness, narrow phantoms conjured before my eyes as if from inside the metal itself. Caged by its circumference, they seemed to goad me with each rotation, their twisted contortions mirroring the smoke grey shapelessness of my fears until I wanted only to close my eyes and tremble.

"Now Dorothy," I scolded myself sometime after midnight: chided for falling victim, yet again, to over-sensitive imagination. "Now Dorothy," I scolded myself, in the same tone that William would use.

I know he slept well last night. I could hear his snores through our fragile dividing wall. Dove Cottage, a public house before it became a home, is hardly built for privacy. I have lain awake before while listening to that rhythm, a waking witness to William's dreams. Every sigh carries with it the whisper of a nasal inflection, about which only Coleridge dares to tease him (one reason, I think, why he prefers the written word to the spoken one).

And yet even without the sound travelling through our weakly plastered partition, even without the inevitable intimacy that grows between two heartbeats sharing a single hearth, I could have predicted that William would rest easy last night. He has an admirable aptitude for composing himself. Self-possession, one might call it, a cerebral sort of dignity that is refined, even set into relief, by excitement or adversity. I admire it. Aspire to it. After all, who would wish to lie sleepless on the night before their wedding? It is fortunate, then, that today is William's wedding day. William's wedding day and not my own.

Now, coaxed into courage by the silverish promise of dawn, I allow my feet to creep out from beneath their covers. My bare soles press against the cool, black-nailed floorboards. A hidden pulse behind my tight, tired eyes throbs in time with every step. Toes curled apologetically, silencing my movements as best I can (noise travels both ways through these walls), I glide towards the window. The ring bucks and twists inside my clenched hand as I move. Angry, it feels to me. Indignant. As if it knows that I am not its rightful owner.

To calm it — at least, to calm myself — I lay my hand on top of the cool stone sill. Grasmere stone is unmistakable, once one learns to look closely: a grey slate veined with white and blue that forms an almost perfect match for the wool of our local Herdwick sheep. Those flat-faced, placid herds command prices at market that I could scarcely comprehend when we first arrived in the village, yet I think I understand something of the attraction now. Their colour is emblematic, a distinctive Grasmere grey seen in the fleeces of shearlings and the shingles of buildings, in the rivulets of hill crags and the sheen of the lake at dusk. Only the yellow steeple at the Church of St Oswald dares to be different.

We prayed there yesterday. I should say that I prayed, while William wrote: rejecting the regular piety of the congregation in favour of a spirituality all of his own. His irreverent, spiderish scribbles were inked down covertly, mid-hymn and even mid-sermon, on whatever scraps of paper he could find within his pockets. Eyes opened — my ears are attuned to the tell-tale scratch of his nib — I knelt to collect a few fragments that had fallen from our pew onto the floor. I'll transcribe them later, I thought. And I did. I always do.

The interior of St Oswald's may seem unremarkable, even undistinguished, but outside the building is vibrant, aglow as if ordained by sunshine in a shade somewhere between goldfinch and kingcup. Visitors to the village may occasionally call it daffodil yellow, but it is a description that I would never choose. The church is steadfast. Solid. Tangible. A daffodil is translucent: its fleeting glimmer comes from within and it flowers, in a glance, just once a year. If damaged, its stem is delicate enough to drift along with the wind, seeds scattered over the shoreline by the carefree whims of stronger currents. A daffodil can be moved according to the wishes of another. And she knows it. It's there, I think, in the way that her petals quiver when touched. It's there in the way she bows her head.

"Sister?" William opens my bedroom door wide. The autumn air follows him inside. "My dear little Dolly. Is it done?" I nod. He takes my hand. The gold ring slips off. Suddenly docile, the metal gleams up at him, pacified and illuminated by light from the windowpane. William's smile glints with it. "From one Wordsworth woman to another." His vivid blue eyes (mine are only slate grey) look animated with anticipation; his face flushed, almost feverish, in his excitement to begin the new day. He stands squarely on the threshold, tall and broad compared with me, and yet somehow a part of him has already left my small, silent room. His presence of mind is too large to linger long within the confines of where domestic duties reside. He kisses the wedding band. Kisses my cheek. "We'll be so happy," he calls out as he leaves me, forgetting to shut my door behind him. "The three of us!" Five of us, I think. Thinking, as I have all night, of Annette and Caroline.

I had never been to France before. William led the way throughout our journey. I followed him without question as we moved from port to port, travelling under the cover of nightfall and, for me, beneath the blinkers of blind trust. Naïve. That is the most accurate word for it. No English counterpart comes close. I felt naïve when William brought me face to face with a woman who — dark eyed and disarmingly beautiful — seemed to be everything I am not. Annette and William claimed a corner of our rented, ill-lit room to converse in, their agitated bursts of speech churning between l'anglais and le français until my mind felt like a vessel poorly equipped for its crossing. Instead, I bent down to be beside the child. A delicate featured girl who carried a simple rag doll. She looked no more than nine years old (ten, I calculated later, with help from my brother's confession). Her eyes, almond shaped and long lashed, were unmistakably her mother's. Her nose, small and yet with a distinctive curve below its bridge, was unmistakably William's.

"Comment tu t'appelles?"

"Caroline." My brother's smile flickered over the child's face.

"Et ta poupée?" Voice weak with shock, I gestured to the rag toy in her arms.

"Dorothy." Caroline offered the doll's face up to me with pride. "Elle port le nom de ma tante." She has the name of my aunt.

*

I listen to the thick thud of William's boots as he hurries down the cottage stairs, an impatient beat that ripples back up our thin walls even as the echo itself withdraws. Mary's feet will be lighter. I know her steps already. My closest friend Mary, soon to be my sister-in-law Mary, and from the day that they announced their engagement, I have dreamed Mary will be like the sister I never had. William is already the brother I lacked for so long. In our childhood — my childhood, I should say — motherless meant becoming brotherless too:

88

the half relatives to whom we were entrusted deciding that my femininity was a blessing (or a burden) to be borne in isolation. With a birthday that falls on Christmas Day, there is only one day a year, rather than two, to remind others of your absence.

Those years may grow into a decade. The girl may grow into a woman. Yet after surviving in the shadows of solitude for so long, I find that my loyalty to the man who finally gave me a home remains resolute. Whatever he does. Whatever he has done. Last night, when William asked me to bless Mary's wedding ring, I obeyed him, but unbidden my mind began to write its own words: the same words for which, I realise now, I was searching inside the gilded walls of St Oswald's. A blessing for Mary. A blessing for myself. A blessing for the French woman to whom I can only ever write, in the hope that my letters cross the Channel. A blessing for the petite niece I will never see grow up. A blessing, each time, from one Wordsworth woman to another.

Downstairs, William lets the cottage door fall shut. Its antiquated hinges shudder, too old to withstand his enthusiasm, and in every reverberation there is the sound of my brother's feet, a crunch over the stones that diminishes until only the trill of birdsong remains. My own descent is slower. More careful. I drift over each stair cautiously; even alone, the habit of not disturbing composition is a difficult one to break. Outside, the autumn winds are forceful, whipping up swirls of discarded leaves that hook onto the hem of my skirt, and each gust conveys that strange, lyrical call of the nearby Herdwicks bleating. Their tufted woollen forms are dotted over the mountainsides, the hills themselves cragged and gnarled like ancient tree roots or growing ivy. I raise my left hand, wriggling my bare ring finger and exposing it to the air. Beneath my feet, the daffodil bulbs are still sheltering under the soil. Alive, if only just, their voices muffled by the earth. Ever glancing, ever changing. Potential bound in bud.

*

'I never saw daffodils so beautiful... they grew among the mossy stones about & about them. Some rested their heads upon these stones as on a pillow for weariness, & the rest tossed & reeled & danced & seemed as if they verily laughed with the wind that blew upon them over the Lake... ever glancing, ever changing.'

Dorothy Wordsworth, *The Grasmere Journal*, 15th April 1802.

'I wandered lonely as a cloud
That floats on high o'er vales and hills,
When all at once I saw a crowd,
A host, of golden daffodils;
Beside the lake, beneath the trees,
Fluttering and dancing in the breeze.'

William Wordsworth, *I Wandered Lonely as a Cloud*, 1804.

Short Story Second Prize

Shirley Gillan
A Loop of Faith

How do I know that I'm still alive? I'm inexperienced in matters of death. In matters of life as well, it turns out. I'd kick myself with the legs that brought me in here, punch myself with the arms that pulled me on, but can't seem to locate them. My nose starts to water with my eyes but I'm unable to lift a hand to wipe either.

From breath to death.

Is it an obvious departure?

Will that be the only border I cross on this, my final trip?

It began with such promise. Has it all been for nothing? Everything about to be snuffed out with a final grasp for air in this unholy place. Not a candle to mark my passing; not a flame to guide my way.

I want to yell and scream. What was that line — do not go gently into the night? Not very Buddhist. This doesn't feel gentle but I cannot rage. I struggle to draw breath, so words, whispered or frenzied, are beyond me. And we were told it's dangerous to make any noise at all, that we must stay quiet, be invisible, until the door is opened on the other side.

What other side am I now talking about?

Did I say that out loud? What if I am raging, unawares, and blow any chance we have left?

I want to find my phone, press a button for a flash of relief from this dark, access a map to see where I am.

Ask Siri if I am alive.

I feel as if I'm being swallowed by an ocean.

Maybe I am already dead.

Shall I just accept it and let myself sink? Drowning all my father's hopes as I go?

It was Hun Ma who first told us, returning from the city with a grin and an offer, just as our rice was glistening emerald in the fields. Jobs and money he said. A chance to escape the poverty we'd all had enough of, bellies empty on our sleep mats, kids crying in their dreams from stomachs cramping in complaint. A year he said. Sell a bit of land for the ticket, get to the UK, work till your pockets are full and come back, rich. Build a new house, feed the whole family forever he said.

Escape, work, return, rebuild. Bloom like a lotus.

He said.

I remember my father and I looking at each other over the grain-dense stalks, feet sinking in eddied earth, a harvest more hopeful than for a long time.

He and I talked into the night, I, for once, the cautious one. My father was convinced and persuasive: Hun Ma has offered us a good deal. We only need to give up half our land, and we don't even need to sell it, as Hun Ma's uncle will take it from us and arrange everything. Travel, passport, visas, work. The work sounded good, growing crops indoors in England, crops that were like diamonds, crops that would change our lives, and I could return after twelve months, pockets and belly full, and buy back our land.

I wanted to share my father's enthusiasm, respond to the light in his eyes that had been dim since my mother passed.

He'd always intended a better life for me. To leave the endless tilling and tending of fields and go to the city and study, or at least work in a job that didn't involve being ankle deep in mud. But he'd crumpled after my mother died and I had stayed. He felt guilty, and saw this as the opportunity I'd missed, the chance for him to make up to me for what he thought I'd lost.

So he'd done it. Handed over a chunk of his only lifeline. And once it had happened, and I was saying farewell to him, to our village, to our country and our continent, I started to feel hopeful. Buoyed up by those I travelled with, united in optimism.

Is this where all that ends?

The night before whenever we're at now, we sat huddled in the woods in Calais, our faces glinting grins in the firelight. It was cold, our only blankets the branches blurring the sky above us, but we didn't mind. We'd got this far. Britain was just a stretch of water, a short tunnel, away.

We'd practically arrived.

Dmitri had come. I'd lost count of the number of contacts and agents we'd dealt with on our six month journey. He was personally going to travel with us, to make sure everything went according to plan he said. We'd travel in a container on the back of a lorry, it was all organised. We didn't need to stand by the motorway, looking for an opportunity to scramble onto a vehicle only to be beaten back off it like most people he said. We were the lucky ones. It was all arranged for us to meet in a carpark where the lorry would pick us up. It would be cold as it was a refrigerated container, but this guaranteed success as we wouldn't be detected by heat sensors at the border. And it was only for a few hours he said. We just had to hand over our passports, anything containing our names, and he would use these to get our work visas all ready for us on the other side. All would be well.

He said.

People plunged hands deep into pockets and handed over their only valuable possession. Evidence of their existence.

My unease began then.

I should have listened to it. But when I mentioned it to Jin, who I'd become close to on the journey, he assured me that they'd brought us this far, sorted everything out — man, how many borders had we successfully crossed? How many modes of transport had we used? — that I pushed it down and handed my passport over. Dmitri gave me a look as he took it — mockery? guilt? — but with that look my unease returned.

What if something went wrong? Was no one else concerned that we were being put inside a travelling fridge? What if we froze or suffocated? No one would know who we were. As it was, anyone we met assumed we were Chinese. My father would spend the rest of his life thinking I'd deserted him, left him to toil our shrunken land alone.

I'd felt sick and left the others, to find a quiet place in the forest, a place with no figures hunched over sparse twigs lit against the cold.

As I unhooked my belt to relieve the cramps in my gut, I felt bad that I'd never got round to mending the frayed lining. It was all I had of my father.

On our last day together he and I had wandered the fields. He'd looked at the large swathe of land that was no longer ours, gold right there in the ripening. As the sun warmed our scalps and a papery rustle swept the swollen crops, my father took off his belt, which had circled the waist of his father before him. This strip of leather, worn smooth by two generations, about to be passed to a third. Tears filled my eyes as I clasped my father's shoulders. I knew he was giving me part of his history. Part of himself. A simple belt, but one that held our family together.

As he'd wrapped it round my waist I could feel the warmth of him.

There was only slight warmth in it as I clasped it in my chilled fingers and pulled it from my waist. I tore a piece from a leaflet detailing times of hot food distribution and, in the light of my phone, wrote my name, village and province as clearly as my numb fingers allowed. I folded the strip as small as I could and pushed it into the gap in the lining, and, muttering an incantation, a prayer, for hope, for safety, for discovery, put the belt back on.

I assume it's still curved around me. It's not warm now.

I hear ragged intakes of breath, but don't know if they're mine. I sense a heaviness across my back — someone else's limb? Reaching out to try to catch my attention? Or is it just me sinking deeper?

Occasional faint warmth tinges the chill on my face, then fades again. Is there someone still breathing next to me? Or is there a hell after all and I am crossing into its heat?

Who else was with me? I was beside Jin when we got on. We'd crouched together behind some crates. The last thing I saw, before the black dropped like a shroud, was Dmitri giving us a thumbs up as he slammed the container shut. Jin had grabbed my arm as the bolt clattered across, but I couldn't see his face to know if it was in excitement or fear. For a moment there was a blank silence, then the hum from the chiller kicked in.

We hardly dared move, we didn't utter a word, so terrified were we of being discovered. We were so close to our destination, we didn't want anything to stop us reaching it.

Even when the chill reached our organs, and the air began to fade, we stayed silent.

There could be no sound.

There is no sound.

Short Story Third Prize

INDEX